'But the true reason
for Babette's presence
in the two sisters'
house was to be
found further back
in time and deeper
down in the domain
of human hearts'

ISAK DINESEN (KAREN BLIXEN)
Born 17 April 1885, Rungsted, Zealand, Denmark
Died 7 September 1962, Rungsted, Zealand, Denmark

Babette's Feast first published in 1958 in the collection
of short stories, *Anecdotes of Destiny*.

ALSO PUBLISHED BY PENGUIN BOOKS
Seven Gothic Tales · Out of Africa · Winter's Tales ·
The Angelic Avengers · Anecdotes of Destiny · Shadows on the Grass

ISAK DINESEN
(KAREN BLIXEN)

Babette's Feast

PENGUIN BOOKS

PENGUIN CLASSICS

Published by the Penguin Group
Penguin Books Ltd, 80 Strand, London WC2R ORL, England
Penguin Group (USA) Inc., 375 Hudson Street, New York, New York 10014, USA
Penguin Group (Canada), 90 Eglinton Avenue East, Suite 700, Toronto, Ontario,
Canada M4P 2Y3 (a division of Pearson Penguin Canada Inc.)
Penguin Ireland, 25 St Stephen's Green, Dublin 2, Ireland (a division of Penguin Books Ltd)
Penguin Group (Australia), 250 Camberwell Road, Camberwell, Victoria 3124, Australia
(a division of Pearson Australia Group Pty Ltd)
Penguin Books India Pvt Ltd, 11 Community Centre, Panchsheel Park,
New Delhi – 110 017, India
Penguin Group (NZ), 67 Apollo Drive, Rosedale, North Shore 0632, New Zealand
(a division of Pearson New Zealand Ltd)
Penguin Books (South Africa) (Pty) Ltd, 24 Sturdee Avenue, Rosebank, Johannesburg 2196,
South Africa

Penguin Books Ltd, Registered Offices: 80 Strand, London WC2R ORL, England

www.penguin.com

Selected from *Anecdotes of Destiny*, published in Penguin Classics 2001
This edition published in Penguin Classics 2011
4

Typeset by Jouve (UK), Milton Keynes
Printed in England by Clays Ltd, St Ives plc

ISBN: 978-0-141-19593-3

www.greenpenguin.co.uk

Babette's Feast

I Two Ladies of Berlevaag

In Norway there is a fjord – a long narrow arm of the sea between tall mountains – named Berlevaag Fjord. At the foot of the mountains the small town of Berlevaag looks like a child's toy-town of little wooden pieces painted gray, yellow, pink and many other colors.

Sixty-five years ago two elderly ladies lived in one of the yellow houses. Other ladies at that time wore a bustle, and the two sisters might have worn it as gracefully as any of them, for they were tall and willowy. But they had never possessed any article of fashion; they had dressed demurely in gray or black all their lives. They were christened Martine and Philippa, after Martin Luther and his friend Philip Melanchton. Their father had been a Dean and a prophet, the founder of a pious ecclesiastic party or sect, which was known and looked up to in all the country of Norway. Its members renounced the pleasures of this world, for the earth and all that it held to them was but a kind of illusion, and the true reality was the New Jerusalem toward which they were longing. They swore not at all, but their communication was yea yea and nay nay, and they called one another Brother and Sister.

The Dean had married late in life and by now had long been dead. His disciples were becoming fewer in number every year, whiter or balder and harder of hearing; they were even becoming somewhat querulous and quarrelsome, so that sad little schisms would arise in the congregation. But they still gathered together to read and interpret the Word. They had all known the Dean's daughters as little girls; to them they were even now very small sisters, precious for their dear father's sake. In the yellow house they felt that their Master's spirit was with them; here they were at home and at peace.

These two ladies had a French maid-of-all-work, Babette.

It was a strange thing for a couple of Puritan women in a small Norwegian town; it might even seem to call for an explanation. The people of Berlevaag found the explanation in the sisters' piety and kindness of heart. For the old Dean's daughters spent their time and their small income in works of charity; no sorrowful or distressed creature knocked on their door in vain. And

Babette had come to that door twelve years ago as a friendless fugitive, almost mad with grief and fear.

But the true reason for Babette's presence in the two sisters' house was to be found further back in time and deeper down in the domain of human hearts.

II Martine's Lover

As young girls, Martine and Philippa had been extra-ordinarily pretty, with the almost supernatural fairness of flowering fruit trees or perpetual snow. They were never to be seen at balls or parties, but people turned when they passed in the streets, and the young men of Berlevaag went to church to watch them walk up the aisle. The younger sister also had a lovely voice, which on Sundays filled the church with sweetness. To the Dean's congregation earthly love, and marriage with it, were trivial matters, in themselves nothing but illusions; still it is possible that more than one of the elderly Brothers had been prizing the maidens far above rubies and had suggested as much to their father. But the Dean had declared that to him in his calling his daughters were his right and left hand. Who could want to bereave him of them? And the fair girls had been brought up to an ideal of heavenly love; they were all filled with it and

3

did not let themselves be touched by the flames of this world.

All the same they had upset the peace of heart of two gentlemen from the great world outside Berlevaag.

There was a young officer named Lorens Loewenhielm, who had led a gay life in his garrison town and had run into debt. In the year of 1854, when Martine was eighteen and Philippa seventeen, his angry father sent him on a month's visit to his aunt in her old country house of Fossum near Berlevaag, where he would have time to meditate and to better his ways. One day he rode into town and met Martine in the marketplace. He looked down at the pretty girl, and she looked up at the fine horseman. When she had passed him and disappeared he was not certain whether he was to believe his own eyes.

In the Loewenhielm family there existed a legend to the effect that long ago a gentleman of the name had married a Huldre, a female mountain spirit of Norway, who is so fair that the air round her shines and quivers. Since then, from time to time, members of the family had been second-sighted. Young Lorens till now had not been aware of any particular spiritual gift in his own nature. But at this one moment there rose before his eyes a sudden, mighty vision of a higher and purer life, with no creditors, dunning letters or parental lectures, with no secret, unpleasant pangs of conscience and with a gentle, golden-haired angel to guide and reward him.

Through his pious aunt he got admission to the Dean's house, and saw that Martine was even lovelier without a bonnet. He followed her slim figure with adoring eyes, but he loathed and despised the figure which he himself cut in her nearness. He was amazed and shocked by the fact that he could find nothing at all to say, and no inspiration in the glass of water before him. 'Mercy and Truth, dear brethren, have met together,' said the Dean. 'Righteousness and Bliss have kissed one another.' And the young man's thoughts were with the moment when Lorens and Martine should be kissing each other. He repeated his visit time after time, and each time seemed to himself to grow smaller and more insignificant and contemptible.

When in the evening he came back to his aunt's house he kicked his shining riding-boots to the corners of his room; he even laid his head on the table and wept.

On the last day of his stay he made a last attempt to communicate his feelings to Martine. Till now it had been easy for him to tell a pretty girl that he loved her, but the tender words stuck in his throat as he looked into this maiden's face. When he had said good-bye to the party, Martine saw him to the door with a candle-stick in her hand. The light shone on her mouth and threw upwards the shadows of her long eyelashes. He was about to leave in dumb despair when on the thresh-old he suddenly seized her hand and pressed it to his lips.

'I am going away forever!' he cried. 'I shall never, never see you again! For I have learned here that Fate is hard, and that in this world there are things which are impossible!'

When he was once more back in his garrison town he thought his adventure over, and found that he did not like to think of it at all. While the other young offi-cers talked of their love affairs, he was silent on his. For seen from the officers' mess, and so to say with its eyes, it was a pitiful business. How had it come to pass that a lieutenant of the hussars had let himself be defeated and frustrated by a set of long-faced sectarians, in the bare-floored rooms of an old Dean's house?

Then he became afraid; panic fell upon him. Was it the family madness which made him still carry with him the dream-like picture of a maiden so fair that she made the air round her shine with purity and holiness? He did not want to be a dreamer; he wanted to be like his brother-officers.

So he pulled himself together, and in the greatest effort of his young life made up his mind to forget what had happened to him in Berlevaag. From now on, he resolved, he would look forward, not back. He would concentrate on his career, and the day was to come when he would cut a brilliant figure in a brilliant world.

His mother was pleased with the result of his visit to Fossum, and in her letters expressed her gratitude to his aunt. She did not know by what queer, winding roads her son had reached his happy moral standpoint.

The ambitious young officer soon caught the attention of his superiors and made unusually quick advancement. He was sent to France and to Russia, and on his return he married a lady-in-waiting to Queen Sophia. In these high circles he moved with grace and ease, pleased with his surroundings and with himself. He even in the course of time benefited from words and turns which had stuck in his mind from the Dean's house, for piety was now in fashion at Court.

In the yellow house of Berlevaag, Philippa sometimes turned the talk to the handsome, silent young man who had so suddenly made his appearance, and so suddenly disappeared again. Her elder sister would then answer her gently, with a still, clear face, and find other things to discuss.

III Philippa's Lover

A year later a more distinguished person even than Lieutenant Loewenhielm came to Berlevaag.

The great singer Achille Papin of Paris had sung for a week at the Royal Opera of Stockholm, and had carried away his audience there as everywhere. One evening a lady of the Court, who had been dreaming of a romance with the artist, had described to him the wild, grandiose scenery of Norway. His own romantic nature was stirred by the narration, and he had laid his way back to France round the Norwegian coast. But he felt small in the sublime surroundings; with nobody to talk to he fell into that melancholy in which he saw himself as an old man, at the end of his career, till on a Sunday, when he could think of nothing else to do, he went to church and heard Philippa sing.

Then in one single moment he knew and understood all. For here were the snowy summits, the wild flowers and the white Nordic nights, translated into his own language of music, and brought him in a young woman's voice. Like Lorens Loewenhielm he had a vision.

'Almighty God,' he thought, 'Thy power is without end, and Thy mercy reacheth unto the clouds! And here is a prima donna of the opera who will lay Paris at her feet.'

Achille Papin at this time was a handsome man of forty, with curly black hair and a red mouth. The idolization of nations had not spoilt him; he was a kind-hearted person and honest toward himself.

He went straight to the yellow house, gave his name – which told the Dean nothing – and explained that he was staying in Berlevaag for his health, and the while would be happy to take on the young lady as a pupil.

He did not mention the Opera of Paris, but described at length how beautifully Miss Philippa would come to sing in church, to the glory of God.

For a moment he forgot himself, for when the Dean asked whether he was a Roman Catholic he answered according to truth, and the old clergyman, who had never seen a live Roman Catholic, grew a little pale. All the same the Dean was pleased to speak French, which reminded him of his young days when he had studied the works of the great French Lutheran writer, Lefèvre d'Etaples. And as nobody could long withstand Achille Papin when he had really set his heart on a matter, in the end the father gave his consent, and remarked to his daughter: 'God's paths run across the sea and the snowy mountains, where man's eye sees no track.'

So the great French singer and the young Norwegian novice set to work together. Achille's expectation grew into certainty and his certainty into ecstasy. He thought: 'I have been wrong in believing that I was growing old. My greatest triumphs are before me! The world will once more believe in miracles when she and I sing together!'

After a while he could not keep his dreams to himself, but told Philippa about them.

She would, he said, rise like a star above any diva of the past or present. The Emperor and Empress, the Princes, great ladies and *bels esprits* of Paris would listen to her, and shed tears. The common people too would worship her, and she would bring consolation and strength to the wronged and oppressed. When she left the Grand Opera upon her master's arm, the crowd would unharness her horses, and themselves draw her to the Café Anglais, where a magnificent supper awaited her.

Philippa did not repeat these prospects to her father or her sister, and this was the first time in her life that she had had a secret from them.

The teacher now gave his pupil the part of Zerlina in Mozart's opera *Don Giovanni* to study. He himself, as often before, sang Don Giovanni's part.

He had never in his life sung as now. In the duet of the second act – which is called the seduction duet – he was swept off his feet by the heavenly music and the heavenly voices. As the last melting note died away he seized Philippa's hands, drew her toward him and kissed her solemnly, as a bridegroom might kiss his bride before the altar. Then he let her go. For the moment was too sublime for any further word or movement; Mozart himself was looking down on the two.

Philippa went home, told her father that she did not want any more singing lessons and asked him to write and tell Monsieur Papin so.

The Dean said: 'And God's paths run across the rivers, my child.'

When Achille got the Dean's letter he sat immovable for an hour. He thought: 'I have been wrong. My day is over. Never again shall I be the divine Papin. And this poor weedy garden of the world has lost its nightingale!'

A little later he thought: 'I wonder what is the matter with that hussy? Did I kiss her, by any chance?'

In the end he thought: 'I have lost my life for a kiss, and I have no remembrance at all of the kiss! Don Giovanni kissed Zerlina, and Achille Papin pays for it! Such is the fate of the artist!'

In the Dean's house Martine felt that the matter was deeper than it looked, and searched her sister's face. For a moment, slightly trembling, she too imagined that the Roman Catholic gentleman might have tried to kiss Philippa. She did not imagine that her sister might have been surprised and frightened by something in her own nature.

Achille Papin took the first boat from Berlevaag.

Of this visitor from the great world the sisters spoke but little; they lacked the words with which to discuss him.

IV A Letter from Paris

Fifteen years later, on a rainy June night of 1871, the bell-rope of the yellow house was pulled violently three times. The mistresses of the house opened the door to a massive, dark, deadly pale woman with a bundle on her arm, who stared at them, took a step forward and fell down on the doorstep in a dead swoon. When the frightened ladies had restored her to life she sat up, gave them one more glance from her sunken eyes and, all the time without a word, fumbled in her wet clothes and brought out a letter which she handed to them.

The letter was addressed to them all right, but it was written in French. The sisters put their heads together and read it. It ran as follows:

Ladies!

Do you remember me? Ah, when I think of you I have the heart filled with wild lilies-of-the-valley! Will the memory of a Frenchman's devotion bend your hearts to save the life of a Frenchwoman?

The bearer of this letter, Madame Babette Hersant, like my beautiful Empress herself, has had to flee from Paris. Civil war has raged in our streets. French hands have shed French blood. The noble Communards, standing up for the Rights of Man, have been crushed and annihilated. Madame Hersant's husband and son, both eminent ladies' hairdressers, have been shot. She herself was arrested as a Pétroleuse – (which word is used here for women who set fire to houses with petroleum) – and has narrowly escaped the blood-stained hands of General Galliffet. She has lost all she possessed and dares not remain in France.

A nephew of hers is cook to the boat *Anna Colbioernsson*, bound for Christiania – (as I believe, the capital of Norway) – and he has obtained shipping opportunity for his aunt. This is now her last sad resort!

Knowing that I was once a visitor to your magnificent country she comes to me, asks me if there be any good people in Norway and begs me, if it be so, to supply her with a letter to them. The two words of 'good people' immediately bring before my eyes your picture, sacred to my heart. I send her to you. How she is to get from Christiania to Berlevaag I know not, having forgotten the map of Norway. But she is a Frenchwoman, and you will find that in her misery she has still got resourcefulness, majesty and true stoicism.

I envy her in her despair: she is to see your faces.

As you receive her mercifully, send a merciful thought back to France.

For fifteen years, Miss Philippa, I have grieved that your voice should never fill the Grand Opera of Paris. When tonight I think of you, no doubt surrounded by a gay and loving family, and of myself: gray, lonely, forgotten by those who once applauded and adored me, I feel that you may have chosen the better part in life. What is fame? What is glory? The grave awaits us all!

And yet, my lost Zerlina, and yet, soprano of the snow! As I write this I feel that the grave is not the end. In Paradise I shall hear your voice again. There you will sing, without fears or scruples, as God meant you to sing. There you will be the great artist that God meant you to be. Ah! how you will enchant the angels.

Babette can cook.

Deign to receive, my ladies, the humble homage of the friend who was once

Achille Papin

At the bottom of the page, as a P.S. were neatly printed the first two bars of the duet between Don Giovanni and Zerlina, like this:

The two sisters till now had kept only a small servant of fifteen to help them in the house and they felt that they could not possibly afford to take on an elderly, experienced housekeeper. But Babette told them that she would serve Monsieur Papin's good people for nothing, and that she would take service with nobody else. If they sent her away she must die. Babette remained in the house of the Dean's daughters for twelve years, until the time of this tale.

V Still Life

Babette had arrived haggard and wild-eyed like a hunted animal, but in her new, friendly surroundings she soon acquired all the appearance of a respectable and trusted servant. She had appeared to be a beggar; she turned out to be a conqueror. Her quiet countenance and her steady, deep glance had magnetic qualities; under her eyes things moved, noiselessly, into their proper places.

Her mistresses at first had trembled a little, just as the Dean had once done, at the idea of receiving a Papist under their roof. But they did not like to worry a hard-tried fellow-creature with catechization; neither were they quite sure of their French. They silently agreed that the example of a good Lutheran life would be the best means of converting their servant. In this way Babette's presence in the house became, so to say, a moral spur to its inhabitants.

They had distrusted Monsieur Papin's assertion that Babette could cook. In France, they knew, people ate frogs. They showed Babette how to prepare a split cod and an ale-and-bread-soup; during the demonstration the Frenchwoman's face became absolutely expressionless. But within a week Babette cooked a split cod and an ale-and-bread-soup as well as anybody born and bred in Berlevaag.

The idea of French luxury and extravagance next had alarmed and dismayed the Dean's daughters. The first day after Babette had entered their service they took her before them and explained to her that they were poor and that to them luxurious fare was sinful. Their own food must be as plain as possible; it was the soup-pails and baskets for their poor that signified. Babette nodded her head; as a girl, she informed her ladies, she had been cook to an old priest who was a saint. Upon this the sisters resolved to surpass the French priest in asceticism. And they soon found that from the day when Babette took over the housekeeping its cost was miraculously reduced, and the soup-pails and baskets acquired a new, mysterious power to stimulate and strengthen their poor and sick.

The world outside the yellow house also came to acknowledge Babette's excellence. The refugee never learned to speak the language of her new country, but in her broken Norwegian she beat down the prices of Berlevaag's flintiest tradesmen. She was held in awe on the quay and in the marketplace.

The old Brothers and Sisters, who had first looked askance at the foreign woman in their midst, felt a happy change in their little sisters' life, rejoiced at it and benefited by it. They found that troubles and cares had been conjured away from their existence, and that now they had money to give away, time for the confidences and complaints of their old friends and peace for meditating on heavenly matters. In the course of time not a few of the brotherhood included Babette's name in their prayers, and thanked God for the speechless stranger, the dark Martha in the house of their two fair Marys. The stone which the builders had almost refused had become the headstone of the corner.

The ladies of the yellow house were the only ones to

know that their cornerstone had a mysterious and alarming feature to it, as if it was somehow related to the Black Stone of Mecca, the Kaaba itself.

Hardly ever did Babette refer to her past life. When in early days the sisters had gently condoled her upon her losses, they had been met with that majesty and stoicism of which Monsieur Papin had written. 'What will you ladies?' she had answered, shrugging her shoulders. 'It is Fate.'

But one day she suddenly informed them that she had for many years held a ticket in a French lottery, and that a faithful friend in Paris was still renewing it for her every year. Some time she might win the *grand prix* of ten thousand francs. At that they felt that their cook's old carpetbag was made from a magic carpet; at a given moment she might mount it and be carried off, back to Paris.

And it happened when Martine or Philippa spoke to Babette that they would get no answer, and would wonder if she had even heard what they said. They would find her in the kitchen, her elbows on the table and her temples on her hands, lost in the study of a heavy black book which they secretly suspected to be a popish prayer-book. Or she would sit immovable on the three-legged kitchen chair, her strong hands in her lap and her dark eyes wide open, as enigmatical and fatal as a

Pythia upon her tripod. At such moments they realized that Babette was deep, and that in the soundings of her being there were passions, there were memories and longings of which they knew nothing at all.

A little cold shiver ran through them, and in their hearts they thought: 'Perhaps after all she had indeed been a Pétroleuse.'

VI Babette's Good Luck

The fifteenth of December was the Dean's hundredth anniversary.

His daughters had long been looking forward to this day and had wished to celebrate it, as if their dear father were still among his disciples. Therefore it had been to them a sad and incomprehensible thing that in this last year discord and dissension had been raising their heads in his flock. They had endeavored to make peace, but they were aware that they had failed. It was as if the fine and lovable vigor of their father's personality had been evaporating, the way Hoffmann's anodyne will evaporate when left on the shelf in a bottle without a cork. And his departure had left the door ajar to things hitherto unknown to the two sisters, much younger than his spiritual children. From a past half a century back, when the unshepherded sheep had been running astray in the mountains, uninvited dismal guests pressed through the opening on the heels of the worshippers and seemed to darken the little rooms and to let in the cold. The sins of old Brothers and Sisters came, with late piercing repentance like a toothache, and the sins of others against them came back with bitter resentment, like a poisoning of the blood.

There were in the congregation two old women who before their conversion had spread slander upon each other, and thereby to each other ruined a marriage and an inheritance. Today they could not remember happenings of yesterday or a week ago, but they remembered this forty-year-old wrong and kept going through the ancient accounts; they scowled at each other. There was an old Brother who suddenly called to mind how another Brother, forty-five years ago, had cheated him in a deal; he could have wished to dismiss the matter from his mind, but it stuck there like a deep-seated, festering splinter. There was a gray, honest skipper and a furrowed, pious widow, who in their young days, while she was the wife of another man, had been sweethearts. Of late each had begun to grieve, while shifting the burden of guilt from his own shoulders to those of the other and back again, and to worry about the possible terrible consequences, through all eternity, to himself, brought upon him by one who had pretended to hold him dear. They grew pale at the meetings in the yellow house and avoided each other's eyes.

As the birthday drew nearer, Martine and Philippa felt the responsibility growing heavier. Would their ever-faithful father look down to his daughters and call them by name as unjust stewards? Between them they talked matters over and repeated their father's saying: that God's paths were running even across the salt sea, and the snow-clad mountains, where man's eye sees no track.

One day of this summer the post brought a letter from France to Madame Babette Hersant. This in itself was a surprising thing, for during these twelve years Babette had received no letter. What, her mistresses wondered, could it contain? They took it into the kitchen to watch her open and read it. Babette opened it, read it, lifted her eyes from it to her ladies' faces and told them that her number in the French lottery had come out. She had won ten thousand francs.

The news made such an impression on the two sisters that for a full minute they could not speak a word. They themselves were used to receiving their modest pension in small instalments; it was difficult to them even to imagine the sum of ten thousand francs in a pile. Then they pressed Babette's hand, their own hands trembling a little. They had never before pressed the hand of a person who the moment before had come into possession of ten thousand francs.

After a while they realized that the happenings concerned themselves as well as Babette. The country of France, they felt, was slowly rising before their servant's horizon, and correspondingly their own existence was sinking beneath their feet. The ten thousand francs which made her rich – how poor did they not make the house she had served! One by one old forgotten cares and worries began to peep out at them from the four corners of the kitchen. The congratulations died on their lips, and the two pious women were ashamed of their own silence.

During the following days they announced the news to their friends with joyous faces, but it did them good to see these friends' faces grow sad as they listened to them. Nobody, it was felt in the Brotherhood, could really blame Babette: birds will return to their nests and human beings to the country of their birth. But did that good and faithful servant realize that in going away from Berlevaag she would be leaving many old and poor people in distress? Their little sisters would have no more time for the sick and sorrowful. Indeed, indeed, lotteries were ungodly affairs.

In due time the money arrived through offices in

Christiania and Berlevaag. The two ladies helped Babette to count it, and gave her a box to keep it in. They handled, and became familiar with, the ominous bits of paper.

They dared not question Babette upon the date of her departure. Dared they hope that she would remain with them over the fifteenth of December?

The mistresses had never been quite certain how much of their private conversation the cook followed or understood. So they were surprised when on a September evening Babette came into the drawing room, more humble or subdued than they had ever seen her, to ask a favor. She begged them, she said, to let her cook a celebration dinner on the Dean's birthday.

The ladies had not intended to have any dinner at all. A very plain supper with a cup of coffee was the most sumptuous meal to which they had ever asked any guest to sit down. But Babette's dark eyes were as eager and pleading as a dog's; they agreed to let her have her way. At this the cook's face lighted up.

But she had more to say. She wanted, she said, to cook a French dinner, a real French dinner, for this one time. Martine and Philippa looked at each other. They did not like the idea; they felt that they did not know what it might imply. But the very strangeness of the request disarmed them. They had no arguments wherewith to meet the proposition of cooking a real French dinner.

Babette drew a long sigh of happiness, but still she did not move. She had one more prayer to make. She begged that her mistresses would allow her to pay for the French dinner with her own money.

'No, Babette!' the ladies exclaimed. How could she imagine such a thing? Did she believe that they would allow her to spend her precious money on food and drink – or on them? No, Babette, indeed.

Babette took a step forward. There was something formidable in the move, like a wave rising. Had she stepped forth like this, in 1871, to plant a red flag on a barricade? She spoke, in her queer Norwegian, with classical French eloquence. Her voice was like a song.

Ladies! Had she ever, during twelve years, asked you a favor? No! And why not? Ladies, you who say your prayers every day, can you imagine what it means to a human heart to have no prayer to make? What would Babette have had to pray for? Nothing! Tonight she had a prayer to make, from the bottom of her heart. Do you not then feel tonight, my ladies, that it becomes you to grant it her, with such joy as that with which the good God has granted you your own?

The ladies for a while said nothing. Babette was right; it was her first request these twelve years; very likely it would be her last. They thought the matter over. After all, they told themselves, their cook was now better off than they, and a dinner could make no difference to a person who owned ten thousand francs.

Their consent in the end completely changed Babette. They saw that as a young woman she had been beautiful. And they wondered whether in this hour they themselves had not, for the very first time, become to her the 'good people' of Achille Papin's letter.

VII The Turtle

In November Babette went for a journey.

She had preparations to make, she told her mistresses, and would need a leave of a week or ten days. Her nephew, who had once got her to Christiania, was still sailing to that town; she must see him and talk things over with him. Babette was a bad sailor; she had spoken of her one sea-voyage, from France to Norway, as of the most horrible experience of her life. Now she was strangely collected; the ladies felt that her heart was already in France.

After ten days she came back to Berlevaag.

Had she got things arranged as she wished? the ladies asked. Yes, she answered, she had seen her nephew and given him a list of the goods which he was to bring her from France. To Martine and Philippa this was a dark saying, but they did not care to talk of her departure, so they asked her no more questions.

Babette was somewhat nervous during the next weeks. But one December day she triumphantly announced to her mistresses that the goods had come to Christiania, had been transshipped there, and on this very day had arrived at Berlevaag. She had, she added, engaged an old man with a wheelbarrow to have them conveyed from the harbor to the house.

But what goods, Babette? the ladies asked. Why, Mesdames, Babette replied, the ingredients for the birthday dinner. Praise be to God, they had all arrived in good condition from Paris.

By this time Babette, like the bottled demon of the fairy tale, had swelled and grown to such dimensions that her mistresses felt small before her. They now saw the French dinner coming upon them, a thing of incalculable nature and range. But they had never in their life broken a promise; they gave themselves into their cook's hands.

All the same when Martine saw a barrow load of bottles wheeled into the kitchen, she stood still. She touched the bottles and lifted up one. 'What is there in this bottle, Babette?' she asked in a low voice. 'Not wine?'

'Wine, Madame!' Babette answered. 'No, Madame. It is a Clos Vougeot 1846!' After a moment she added: 'From Philippe, in Rue Montorgueil!' Martine had never suspected that wines could have names to them, and was put to silence.

Late in the evening she opened the door to a ring, and was once more faced with the wheelbarrow, this time with a red-haired sailor-boy behind it, as if the old man had by this time been worn out. The youth grinned at her as he lifted a big, undefinable object from the barrow. In the light of the lamp it looked like some greenish-black stone, but when set down on the kitchen floor it suddenly shot out a snake-like head and moved it slightly from side to side. Martine had seen pictures of tortoises, and had even as a child owned a pet tortoise, but this thing was monstrous in size and terrible to behold. She backed out of the kitchen without a word.

She dared not tell her sister what she had seen. She passed an almost sleepless night; she thought of her father and felt that on his very birthday she and her sister were lending his house to a witches' sabbath. When at last she fell asleep she had a terrible dream, in which she saw Babette poisoning the old Brothers and Sisters, Philippa and herself.

Early in the morning she got up, put on her gray

cloak and went out in the dark street. She walked from house to house, opened her heart to her Brothers and Sisters, and confessed her guilt. She and Philippa, she said, had meant no harm; they had granted their servant a prayer and had not foreseen what might come of it. Now she could not tell what, on her father's birthday, her guests would be given to eat or drink. She did not actually mention the turtle, but it was present in her face and voice.

The old people, as has already been told, had all known Martine and Philippa as little girls; they had seen them cry bitterly over a broken doll. Martine's tears brought tears into their own eyes. They gathered in the afternoon and talked the problem over.

Before they again parted they promised one another that for their little sisters' sake they would, on the great day, be silent upon all matters of food and drink. Nothing that might be set before them, be it even frogs or snails, should wring a word from their lips.

'Even so,' said a white-bearded Brother, 'the tongue is a little member and boasteth great things. The tongue can no man tame; it is an unruly evil, full of deadly poison. On the day of our master we will cleanse our tongues of all taste and purify them of all delight or disgust of the senses, keeping and preserving them for the higher things of praise and thanksgiving.'

So few things ever happened in the quiet existence of the Berlevaag brotherhood that they were at this moment deeply moved and elevated. They shook hands on their vow, and it was to them as if they were doing so before the face of their Master.

VIII The Hymn

On Sunday morning it began to snow. The white flakes fell fast and thick; the small windowpanes of the yellow house became pasted with snow.

Early in the day a groom from Fossum brought the two sisters a note. Old Mrs Loewenhielm still resided in her country house. She was now ninety years old and stone-deaf, and she had lost all sense of smell or taste. But she had been one of the Dean's first supporters, and neither her infirmity nor the sledge journey would keep her from doing honor to his memory. Now, she wrote, her nephew, General Lorens Loewenhielm, had unexpectedly come on a visit; he had spoken with deep veneration of the Dean, and she begged permission to bring him with her. It would do him good, for the dear boy seemed to be in somewhat low spirits.

Martine and Philippa at this remembered the young officer and his visits; it relieved their present anxiety to talk of old happy days. They wrote back that General Loewenhielm would be welcome. They also called in Babette to inform her that they would now be twelve for dinner; they added that their latest guest had lived in Paris for several years. Babette seemed pleased with the news, and assured them that there would be food enough.

The hostesses made their little preparations in the sitting room. They dared not set foot in the kitchen, for Babette had mysteriously nosed out a cook's mate from a ship in the harbor – the same boy, Martine realized, who had brought in the turtle – to assist her in the kitchen and to wait at table, and now the dark woman and the red-haired boy, like some witch with her familiar spirit, had taken possession of these regions. The ladies could not tell what fires had been burning or what cauldrons bubbling there from before daybreak.

Table linen and plate had been magically mangled and polished, glasses and decanters brought, Babette only knew from where. The Dean's house did not possess twelve dining-room chairs, the long horse-hair-covered sofa had been moved from the parlor to the dining room, and the parlor, ever sparsely furnished, now looked strangely bare and big without it.

Martine and Philippa did their best to embellish the domain left to them. Whatever troubles might be in wait for their guests, in any case they should not be cold; all day the sisters fed the towering old stove with birch-knots. They hung a garland of juniper round their father's portrait on the wall, and placed candlesticks on their mother's small working table beneath it; they burned juniper-twigs to make the room smell nice. The while they wondered if in this weather the sledge from Fossum would get through. In the end they put on their old black best frocks and their confirmation gold crosses. They sat down, folded their hands in their laps and committed themselves unto God.

The old Brothers and Sisters arrived in small groups and entered the room slowly and solemnly.

This low room with its bare floor and scanty furniture was dear to the Dean's disciples. Outside its windows lay the great world. Seen from in here the great world in its winter-whiteness was ever prettily bordered in pink, blue and red by the row of hyacinths on the window-sills. And in summer, when the windows were open, the great world had a softly moving frame of white muslin curtains to it.

Tonight the guests were met on the doorstep with warmth and sweet smell, and they were looking into the face of their beloved Master, wreathed with evergreen. Their hearts like their numb fingers thawed.

One very old Brother, after a few moments' silence,

in his trembling voice struck up one of the Master's own hymns:

> *'Jerusalem, my happy home*
> *name ever dear to me . . .'*

One by one the other voices fell in, thin quivering women's voices, ancient seafaring Brothers' deep growls, and above them all Philippa's clear soprano, a little worn with age but still angelic. Unwittingly the choir had seized one another's hands. They sang the hymn to the end, but could not bear to cease and joined in another:

> *'Take not thought for food or raiment*
> *careful one, so anxiously . . .'*

The mistresses of the house somewhat reassured by it, the words of the third verse:

> *'Wouldst thou give a stone, a reptile*
> *to thy pleading child for food? . . .'*

went straight to Martine's heart and inspired her with hope.

In the middle of this hymn sledge bells were heard outside; the guests from Fossum had arrived.

Martine and Philippa went to receive them and saw them into the parlor. Mrs Loewenhielm with age had become quite small, her face colorless like parchment, and very still. By her side General Loewenhielm, tall, broad and ruddy, in his bright uniform, his breast covered with decorations, strutted and shone like an ornamental bird, a golden pheasant or a peacock, in this sedate party of black crows and jackdaws.

IX General Loewenhielm

General Loewenhielm had been driving from Fossum to Berlevaag in a strange mood. He had not visited this part of the country for thirty years. He had come now to get a rest from his busy life at Court, and he had found no rest. The old house of Fossum was peaceful enough and seemed somehow pathetically small after the Tuileries and the Winter Palace. But it held one disquieting figure: young Lieutenant Loewenhielm walked in its rooms.

General Loewenhielm saw the handsome, slim figure pass close by him. And as he passed, the boy gave the elder man a short glance and a smile, the haughty, arrogant smile which youth gives to age. The General might have smiled back, kindly and a little sadly, as age smiles at youth, if it had not been that he was really in no mood to smile; he was, as his aunt had written, in low spirits.

General Loewenhielm had obtained everything that he had striven for in life and was admired and envied by everyone. Only he himself knew of a queer fact, which jarred with his prosperous existence: that he was not perfectly happy. Something was wrong somewhere, and he carefully felt his mental self all over, as one feels a finger over to determine the place of a deep-seated, invisible thorn.

He was in high favor with royalty, he had done well in his calling, he had friends everywhere. The thorn sat in none of these places.

His wife was a brilliant woman and still good-looking. Perhaps she neglected her own house a little for her visits and parties; she changed her servants every three months and the General's meals at home were served unpunctually. The General, who valued good food highly in life, here felt a slight bitterness against the lady, and secretly blamed her for the indigestion from which he sometimes suffered. Still the thorn was not here either.

Nay, but an absurd thing had lately been happening to General Loewenhielm: he would find himself worrying about his immortal soul. Did he have any reason for doing so? He was a moral person, loyal to his king, his wife and his friends, an example to everybody. But there were moments when it seemed to him that the world was not a moral, but a mystic, concern. He looked into the mirror, examined the row of decorations on his breast and sighed to himself: 'Vanity, vanity, all is vanity!'

The strange meeting at Fossum had compelled him to make out the balance-sheet of his life.

Young Lorens Loewenhielm had attracted dreams and fancies as a flower attracts bees and butterflies. He had fought to free himself of them; he had fled and they had followed. He had been scared of the Huldre of the family legend and had declined her invitation to come into the mountain; he had firmly refused the gift of second sight.

The elderly Lorens Loewenhielm found himself wishing that one little dream would come his way, and a gray moth of dusk look him up before nightfall. He found himself longing for the faculty of second sight, as a blind man will long for the normal faculty of vision.

Can the sum of a row of victories in many years and in many countries be a defeat? General Loewenhielm had fulfilled Lieutenant Loewenhielm's wishes and had more than satisfied his ambitions. It might be held that he had gained the whole world. And it had come to this,

that the stately, worldly-wise older man now turned
toward the naïve young figure to ask him, gravely, even
bitterly, in what he had profited? Somewhere something
had been lost.

When Mrs Loewenhielm had told her nephew of the
Dean's anniversary and he had made up his mind to go
with her to Berlevaag, his decision had not been an
ordinary acceptance of a dinner invitation.

He would, he resolved, tonight make up his account
with young Lorens Loewenhielm, who had felt himself
to be a shy and sorry figure in the house of the Dean,
and who in the end had shaken its dust off his riding-
boots. He would let the youth prove to him, once and
for all, that thirty-one years ago he had made the right
choice. The low rooms, the haddock and the glass of
water on the table before him should all be called in to
bear evidence that in their milieu the existence of
Lorens Loewenhielm would very soon have become
sheer misery.

He let his mind stray far away. In Paris he had once
won a *concours hippique* and had been feted by high
French cavalry officers, princes and dukes among them.
A dinner had been given in his honor at the finest res-
taurant of the city. Opposite him at table was a noble
lady, a famous beauty whom he had long been court-
ing. In the midst of dinner she had lifted her dark velvet

eyes above the rim of her champagne glass and without words had promised to make him happy. In the sledge he now all of a sudden remembered that he had then, for a second, seen Martine's face before him and had rejected it. For a while he listened to the tinkling of the sledge bells, then he smiled a little as he reflected how he would tonight come to dominate the conversation round that same table by which young Lorens Loewenhielm had sat mute.

Large snowflakes fell densely; behind the sledge the tracks were wiped out quickly. General Loewenhielm sat immovable by the side of his aunt, his chin sunk in the high fur collar of his coat.

X Babette's Dinner

As Babette's red-haired familiar opened the door to the dining room, and the guests slowly crossed the threshold, they let go one another's hands and became silent. But the silence was sweet, for in spirit they still held hands and were still singing.

Babette had set a row of candles down the middle of the table; the small flames shone on the black coats and frocks and on the one scarlet uniform, and were reflected in clear, moist eyes.

General Loewenhielm saw Martine's face in the candlelight as he had seen it when the two parted, thirty years ago. What traces would thirty years of Berlevaag life have left on it? The golden hair was now streaked with silver; the flower-like face had slowly been turned into alabaster. But how serene was the forehead, how quietly trustful the eyes, how pure and sweet the mouth, as if no hasty word had ever passed its lips.

When all were seated, the eldest member of the congregation said grace in the Dean's own words:

> *'May my food my body maintain,*
> *may my body my soul sustain,*
> *may my soul in deed and word*
> *give thanks for all things to the Lord.'*

At the word of 'food' the guests, with their old heads bent over their folded hands, remembered how they had vowed not to utter a word about the subject, and in their hearts they reinforced the vow: they would not even give it a thought! They were sitting down to a meal, well, so had people done at the wedding of Cana. And grace has chosen to manifest itself there, in the very wine, as fully as anywhere.

Babette's boy filled a small glass before each of the

party. They lifted it to their lips gravely, in confirmation of their resolution.

General Loewenhielm, somewhat suspicious of his wine, took a sip of it, startled, raised the glass first to his nose and then to his eyes, and sat it down bewildered. 'This is very strange!' he thought. 'Amontillado! And the finest Amontillado that I have ever tasted.' After a moment, in order to test his senses, he took a small spoonful of his soup, took a second spoonful and laid down his spoon. 'This is exceedingly strange!' he said to himself. 'For surely I am eating turtle-soup – and what turtle-soup!' He was seized by a queer kind of panic and emptied his glass.

Usually in Berlevaag people did not speak much while they were eating. But somehow this evening tongues had been loosened. An old Brother told the story of his first meeting with the Dean. Another went through that sermon which sixty years ago had brought about his conversion. An aged woman, the one to whom Martine had first confided her distress, reminded her friends how in all afflictions any Brother or Sister was ready to share the burden of any other.

General Loewenhielm, who was to dominate the conversation of the dinner table, related how the Dean's collection of sermons was a favorite book of the

Queen's. But as a new dish was served he was silenced. 'Incredible!' he told himself. 'It is Blinis Demidoff!' He looked round at his fellow-diners. They were all quietly eating their Blinis Demidoff, without any sign of either surprise or approval, as if they had been doing so every day for thirty years.

A Sister on the other side of the table opened on the subject of strange happenings which had taken place while the Dean was still amongst his children, and which one might venture to call miracles. Did they remember, she asked, the time when he had promised a Christmas sermon in the village the other side of the fjord? For a fortnight the weather had been so bad that no skipper or fisherman would risk the crossing. The villagers were giving up hope, but the Dean told them that if no boat would take him, he would come to them walking upon the waves. And behold! Three days before Christmas the storm stopped, hard frost set in, and the fjord froze from shore to shore – and this was a thing which had not happened within the memory of man!

The boy once more filled the glasses. This time the Brothers and Sisters knew that what they were given to drink was not wine, for it sparkled. It must be some kind of lemonade. The lemonade agreed with their exalted state of mind and seemed to lift them off the ground, into a higher and purer sphere.

General Loewenhielm again set down his glass, turned to his neighbor on the right and said to him: 'But surely this is a Veuve Cliquot 1860?' His neighbor looked at him kindly, smiled at him and made a remark about the weather.

Babette's boy had his instructions; he filled the glasses of the Brotherhood only once, but he refilled the General's glass as soon as it was emptied. The General emptied it quickly time after time. For how is a man of sense to behave when he cannot trust his senses? It is better to be drunk than mad.

Most often the people in Berlevaag during the course of a good meal would come to feel a little heavy. Tonight it was not so. The *convives* grew lighter in weight and lighter of heart the more they ate and drank. They no longer needed to remind themselves of their vow. It was, they realized, when man has not only altogether forgotten but has firmly renounced all ideas of food and drink that he eats and drinks in the right spirit.

General Loewenhielm stopped eating and sat immovable. Once more he was carried back to that dinner in Paris of which he had thought in the sledge. An incredibly recherché and palatable dish had been served there; he had asked its name from his fellow diner, Colonel Galliffet, and the Colonel had smilingly told him that it was named 'Cailles en Sarcophage.' He had further told him that the dish had been invented by the chef of the very café in which they were dining, a person known all over Paris as the greatest culinary genius of the age, and – most surprisingly – a woman! 'And indeed,' said Colonel Galliffet, 'this woman is now turning a dinner at the Café Anglais into a kind of love affair – into a love affair of the noble and romantic category in which one no longer distinguishes between bodily and spiritual appetite or satiety! I have, before now, fought a duel for the sake of a fair lady. For no woman in all Paris, my young friend, would I more willingly shed my blood!' General Loewenhielm turned to his neighbor on the left and said to him: 'But this is Cailles en Sarcophage!' The neighbor, who had been listening to the description of a miracle, looked at him absent-mindedly, then nodded his head and answered: 'Yes, Yes, certainly. What else would it be?'

From the Master's miracles the talk round the table had turned to the smaller miracles of kindliness and helpfulness daily performed by his daughters. The old Brother who had first struck up the hymn quoted the Dean's saying: 'The only things which we may take with us from our life on earth are those which we have given away!' The guests smiled – what nabobs would not the poor, simple maidens become in the next world!

General Loewenhielm no longer wondered at anything. When a few minutes later he saw grapes, peaches and fresh figs before him, he laughed to his neighbor across the table and remarked: 'Beautiful grapes!' His neighbor replied: ' "And they came onto the brook of Eshcol, and cut down a branch with one cluster of grapes. And they bare it two upon a staff." '

Then the General felt that the time had come to make a speech. He rose and stood up very straight.

Nobody else at the dinner table had stood up to speak. The old people lifted their eyes to the face above them in high, happy expectation. They were used to seeing sailors and vagabonds dead drunk with the crass gin of the country, but they did not recognize in a warrior and courtier the intoxication brought about by the noblest wine of the world.

XI General Loewenhielm's Speech

'Mercy and truth, my friends, have met together,' said the General. 'Righteousness and bliss shall kiss one another.'

He spoke in a clear voice which had been trained in drill grounds and had echoed sweetly in royal halls, and yet he was speaking in a manner so new to himself and so strangely moving that after his first sentence he had to make a pause. For he was in the habit of forming his speeches with care, conscious of his purpose, but here, in the midst of the Dean's simple congregation, it was as if the whole figure of General Loewenhielm, his breast covered with decorations, were but a mouth-piece for a message which meant to be brought forth.

'Man, my friends,' said General Loewenhielm, 'is frail and foolish. We have all of us been told that grace is to be found in the universe. But in our human foolish-ness and short-sightedness we imagine divine grace to be finite. For this reason we tremble. . .' Never till now had the General stated that he trembled; he was genu-inely surprised and even shocked at hearing his own voice proclaim the fact. 'We tremble before making our choice in life, and after having made it again tremble in fear of having chosen wrong. But the moment comes when our eyes are opened, and we see and realize that grace is infinite. Grace, my friends, demands nothing from us but that we shall await it with confidence and acknowledge it in gratitude. Grace, brothers, makes no conditions and singles out none of us in particular; grace takes us all to its bosom and proclaims general amnesty. See! that which we have chosen is given us, and that which we have refused is, also and at the same time, granted us. Ay, that which we have rejected is poured upon us abundantly. For mercy and truth have met together, and righteousness and bliss have kissed one another!'

The Brothers and Sisters had not altogether understood the General's speech, but his collected and inspired face and the sound of well-known and cherished words had seized and moved all hearts. In this way, after thirty-one years, General Loewenhielm succeeded in dominating the conversation at the Dean's dinner table.

Of what happened later in the evening nothing definite can here be stated. None of the guests later on had any clear remembrance of it. They only knew that the rooms had been filled with a heavenly light, as if a number of small halos had blended into one glorious radiance. Taciturn old people received the gift of tongues; ears that for years had been almost deaf were opened to it. Time itself had merged into eternity. Long after midnight the windows of the house shone like gold, and golden song flowed out into the winter air.

The two old women who had once slandered each other now in their hearts went back a long way, past the evil period in which they had been stuck, to those days of their early girlhood when together they had been preparing for confirmation and hand in hand had filled the roads round Berlevaag with singing. A Brother in the congregation gave another a knock in the ribs, like a rough caress between boys, and cried out: 'You cheated me on that timber, you old scoundrel!' The Brother thus addressed almost collapsed in a heavenly burst of laughter, but tears ran from his eyes. 'Yes, I did so, beloved Brother,' he answered. 'I did so.' Skipper Halvorsen and Madam Oppegaarden suddenly found themselves close together in a corner and gave one another that long, long kiss, for which the secret uncertain love affair of their youth had never left them time.

The old Dean's flock were humble people. When later in life they thought of this evening it never occurred to any of them that they might have been exalted by their own merit. They realized that the infinite grace of which General Loewenhielm had spoken had been allotted to them, and they did not even wonder at the fact, for it had been but the fulfillment of an ever-present hope. The vain illusions of this earth had dissolved before their eyes like smoke, and they had seen the universe as it really is. They had been given one hour of the millennium.

Old Mrs Loewenhielm was the first to leave. Her nephew accompanied her, and their hostesses lighted them out. While Philippa was helping the old lady into her many wraps, the General seized Martine's hand and held it for a long time without a word. At last he said:

'I have been with you every day of my life. You know, do you not, that it has been so?'

'Yes,' said Martine, 'I know that it has been so.'

'And,' he continued, 'I shall be with you every day that is left to me. Every evening I shall sit down, if not in the flesh, which means nothing, in spirit, which is all, to dine with you, just like tonight. For tonight I have learned, dear sister, that in this world anything is possible.'

'Yes, it is so, dear brother,' said Martine. 'In this world anything is possible.'

Upon this they parted.

When at last the company broke up it had ceased to snow. The town and the mountains lay in white, unearthly splendor and the sky was bright with thousands of stars. In the street the snow was lying so deep that it had become difficult to walk. The guests from the yellow house wavered on their feet, staggered, sat down abruptly or fell forward on their knees and hands and were covered with snow, as if they had indeed had their sins washed white as wool, and in this regained innocent attire were gamboling like little lambs. It was, to each of them, blissful to have become as a small child; it was also a blessed joke to watch old Brothers and Sisters, who had been taking themselves so seriously, in this kind of celestial second childhood. They stumbled and got up, walked on or stood still, bodily as well as spiritually hand in hand, at moments performing the great chain of a beatified *lanciers*.

'Bless you, bless you, bless you,' like an echo of the harmony of the spheres rang on all sides.

Martine and Philippa stood for a long time on the stone steps outside the house. They did not feel the cold. 'The stars have come nearer,' said Philippa.

'They will come every night,' said Martine quietly. 'Quite possibly it will never snow again.'

In this, however, she was mistaken. An hour later it again began to snow, and such a heavy snowfall had never been known in Berlevaag. The next morning people could hardly push open their doors against the tall snow-drifts. The windows of the houses were so thickly covered with snow, it was told for years afterwards, that many good citizens of the town did not realize that daybreak had come, but slept on till late in the afternoon.

XII The Great Artist

When Martine and Philippa locked the door they remembered Babette. A little wave of tenderness and pity swept through them: Babette alone had had no share in the bliss of the evening.

So they went out into the kitchen, and Martine said to Babette: 'It was quite a nice dinner, Babette.'

Their hearts suddenly filled with gratitude. They realized that none of their guests had said a single word about the food. Indeed, try as they might, they could not themselves remember any of the dishes which had been served. Martine bethought herself of the turtle. It had not appeared at all, and now seemed very vague and far away; it was quite possible that it had been nothing but a nightmare.

Babette sat on the chopping block, surrounded by more black and greasy pots and pans than her mistresses had ever seen in their life. She was as white and as deadly exhausted as on the night when she first appeared and had fainted on their doorstep.

After a long time she looked straight at them and said: 'I was once cook at the Café Anglais.'

Martine said again: 'They all thought that it was a nice dinner.' And when Babette did not answer a word she added: 'We will all remember this evening when you have gone back to Paris, Babette.'

Babette said: 'I am not going back to Paris.'

'You are not going back to Paris?' Martine exclaimed.

'No,' said Babette. 'What will I do in Paris? They have all gone. I have lost them all, Mesdames.'

The sisters' thoughts went to Monsieur Hersant and his son, and they said: 'Oh, my poor Babette.'

'Yes, they have all gone,' said Babette. 'The Duke of Morny, the Duke of Decazes, Prince Narishkine, General Galliffet, Aurélian Scholl, Paul Daru, the Princesse Pauline! All!'

The strange names and titles of people lost to Babette faintly confused the two ladies, but there was such an infinite perspective of tragedy in her announcement that in their responsive state of mind they felt her losses as their own, and their eyes filled with tears.

At the end of another long silence Babette suddenly smiled slightly at them and said: 'And how would I go back to Paris, Mesdames? I have no money.'

'No money?' the sisters cried as with one mouth.

'No,' said Babette.

'But the ten thousand francs?' the sisters asked in a horrified gasp.

'The ten thousand francs have been spent, Mesdames,' said Babette.

The sisters sat down. For a full minute they could not speak.

'But ten thousand francs?' Martine slowly whispered.

'What will you, Mesdames,' said Babette with great dignity. 'A dinner for twelve at the Café Anglais would cost ten thousand francs.'

The ladies still did not find a word to say. The piece of news was incomprehensible to them, but then many things tonight in one way or another had been beyond comprehension.

Martine remembered a tale told by a friend of her father's who had been a missionary in Africa. He had saved the life of an old chief's favorite wife, and to show his gratitude the chief had treated him to a rich meal. Only long afterwards the missionary learned from his own black servant that what he had partaken of was a small fat grandchild of the chief's, cooked in honor of the great Christian medicine man. She shuddered.

But Philippa's heart was melting in her bosom. It seemed that an unforgettable evening was to be finished off with an unforgettable proof of human loyalty and self-sacrifice.

'Dear Babette,' she said softly, 'you ought not to have given away all you had for our sake.'

Babette gave her mistress a deep glance, a strange glance. Was there not pity, even scorn, at the bottom of it?

'For your sake?' she replied. 'No. For my own.'

She rose from the chopping block and stood up before the two sisters.

'I am a great artist!' she said.

She waited a moment and then repeated: 'I am a great artist, Mesdames.'

Again for a long time there was deep silence in the kitchen.

Then Martine said: 'So you will be poor now all your life, Babette?'

'Poor?' said Babette. She smiled as if to herself. 'No, I shall never be poor. I told you that I am a great artist. A great artist, Mesdames, is never poor. We have something, Mesdames, of which other people know nothing.'

While the elder sister found nothing more to say, in Philippa's heart deep, forgotten chords vibrated. For she had heard, before now, long ago, of the Café Anglais. She had heard, before now, long ago, the names on Babette's tragic list. She rose and took a step toward her servant.

'But all those people whom you have mentioned,' she said, 'those princes and great people of Paris whom you named, Babette? You yourself fought against them. You were a Communard! The General you named had your husband and son shot! How can you grieve over them?'

Babette's dark eyes met Philippa's.

'Yes,' she said, 'I was a Communard. Thanks be to God, I was a Communard! And those people whom I named, Mesdames, were evil and cruel. They let the people of Paris starve; they oppressed and wronged the poor. Thanks be to God, I stood upon a barricade; I loaded the gun for my menfolk! But all the same, Mesdames, I shall not go back to Paris, now that those people of whom I have spoken are no longer there.'

She stood immovable, lost in thought.

'You see, Mesdames,' she said, at last, 'those people belonged to me, they were mine. They had been brought up and trained, with greater expense than you, my little ladies, could ever imagine or believe, to understand what a great artist I am. I could make them happy. When I did my very best I could make them perfectly happy.'

She paused for a moment.

'It was like that with Monsieur Papin too,' she said.

'With Monsieur Papin?' Philippa asked.

'Yes, with your Monsieur Papin, my poor lady,' said Babette. 'He told me so himself: "It is terrible and unbearable to an artist," he said, "to be encouraged to do, to be applauded for doing, his second best." He said: "Through all the world there goes one long cry from the heart of the artist: Give me leave to do my utmost!"'

Philippa went up to Babette and put her arms round her. She felt the cook's body like a marble monument against her own, but she herself shook and trembled from head to foot.

For a while she could not speak. Then she whispered:

'Yet this is not the end! I feel, Babette, that this is not the end. In Paradise you will be the great artist that God meant you to be! Ah!' she added, the tears streaming down her cheeks. 'Ah, how you will enchant the angels!'

a little history

Penguin Modern Classics were launched in 1961, and have been shaping the reading habits of generations ever since.

The list began with distinctive grey spines and evocative pictorial covers – a look that, after various incarnations, continues to influence their current design – and with books that are still considered landmark classics today.

Penguin Modern Classics have caused scandal and political change, inspired great films and broken down barriers, whether social, sexual or the boundaries of language itself. They remain the most provocative, groundbreaking, exciting and revolutionary works of the last 100 years (or so).

In 2011, on the fiftieth anniversary of the Modern Classics, we're publishing fifty Mini Modern Classics: the very best short fiction by writers ranging from Beckett to Conrad, Nabokov to Saki, Updike to Wodehouse. Though they don't take long to read, they'll stay with you long after you turn the final page.